First published in Great Britain in 2015 by Andersen Press Ltd.,
20 Vauxhall Bridge Road, London SW1V 2SA.
Published in Australia by Random House Australia Pty.,
Level 3, 100 Pacific Highway, North Sydney, NSW 2060.
Copyright © Richard Byrne, 2015
The rights of Richard Byrne to be identified as the author and illustrator
of this work have been asserted by him in accordance with the
Copyright, Designs and Patents Act, 1988. All rights reserved.
Colour Separated in Switzerland by Photolitho AG, Zürich.
Printed and bound in Malaysia by Tien Wah Press.
1 3 5 7 9 10 8 6 4 2

British Library Cataloguing in Publication Data available. ISBN 978 1 78344 117 4

www.richardbyrne.co.uk

Other books by Richard Byrne:
PENGUINS CAN'T FLY!

For Max, David, Martin, Teresa, Charlotte and Christopher.

Richard Byrne

Spotty Lottie and Me

Andersen Press

Joey had chicken pox and had to stay at home.
He was **really** missing his friends.

"Being ill is **boring**!" he complained.
"You can play with a friend," said Joey's mummy,
"but they will have to be a spotty one, because
you are still **infectious**."

Joey thought about where he might
find a spotty friend.

Then he had a **good idea!**

"Hello, spotty leopard, will **you** play with me?" he asked.

Leopard took **one look** at Joey and explained that he **had** to be somewhere else.

Joey didn't
have much luck
elsewhere.

Snake said he was **terribly sorry**,
but he was **late** for an appointment
and **had** to skedaddle...

...Cheetah had to dash...

...and **giraffe** didn't
hang around
for long...

Even ladybird said

she had to fly.

"NOBODY WANTS TO PLAY WITH ME!"

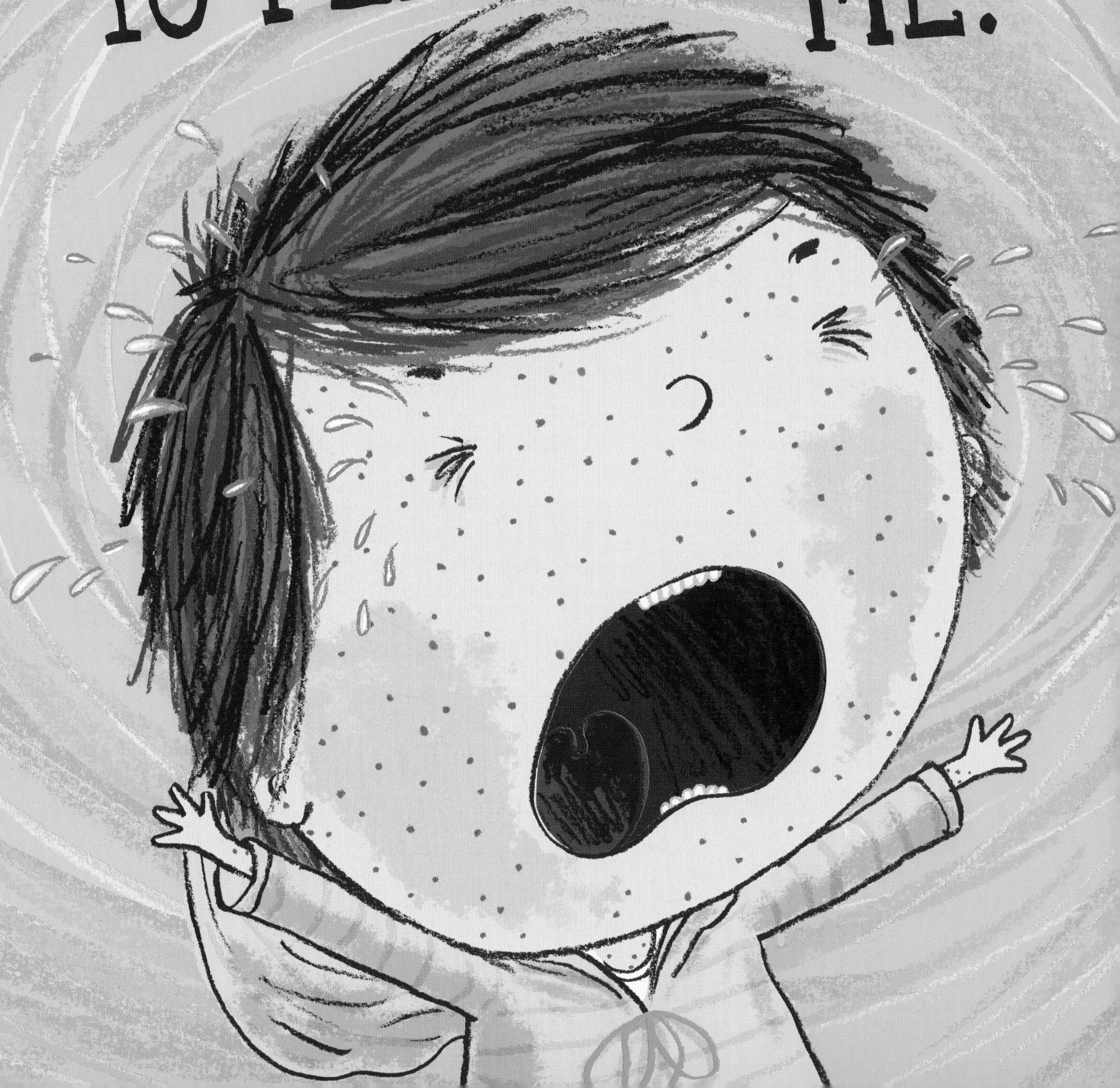

Soon after
Joey returned home,
there was a **knock**
at the **door**.

It was...

...LOTTIE!

"I've got

chicken pox too!"

she said.

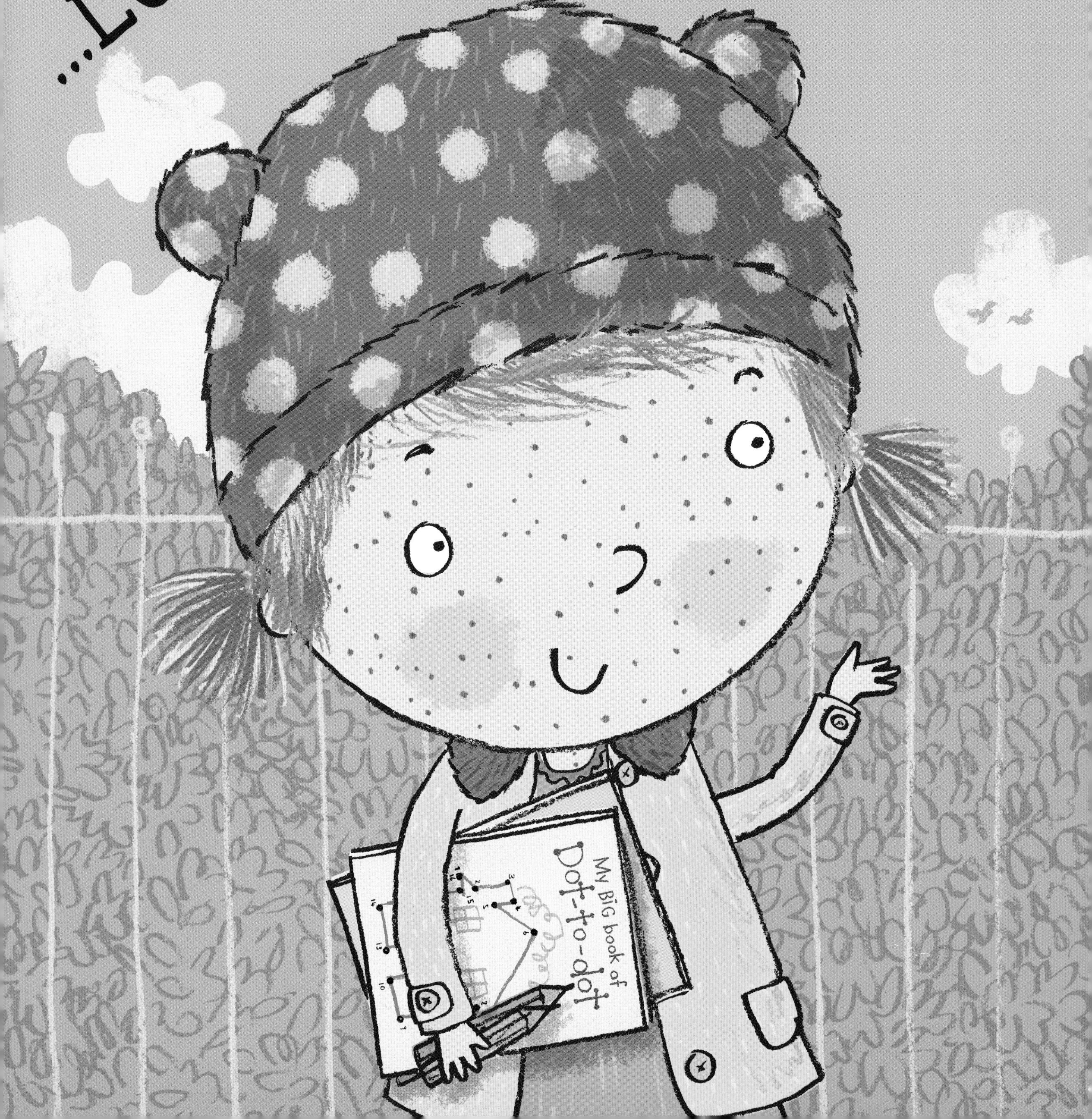

Joey and Lottie had a **lot** of **fun** together
and after a few days...

...their spots
began to disappear.

Now that Joey's spots had gone, all the animals wanted to play too.

But as they came **nearer...**

...and took a closer look at
Joey's face...

"Yuck!"